Start with Art

Prints

Isabel Thomas

www.raintreepublishers.co.uk
Visit our website to find out
more information about
Raintree books.

To order:
☎ Phone 0845 6044371
🖷 Fax +44 (0) 1865 312263
🖳 Email myorders@raintreepublishers.co.uk

Customers from outside the UK please telephone +44 1865 312262

Raintree is an imprint of Capstone Global Library Limited,
a company incorporated in England and Wales having its
registered office at 7 Pilgrim Street, London, EC4V 6LB –
Registered company number: 6695582

Text © Capstone Global Library Limited 2012
First published in hardback in 2012
The moral rights of the proprietor have been asserted.

Edited by Dan Nunn, Rebecca Rissman, and Catherine Veitch
Designed by Richard Parker
Picture research by Mica Brancic and Hannah Taylor
Originated by Capstone Global Library
Printed and bound in China by South China Printing
   Company Ltd

ISBN 978 1 406 22409 2
15 14 13 12 11
10 9 8 7 6 5 4 3 2 1

British Library Cataloguing in Publication Data
Thomas, Isabel
Prints. -- (Start with art)
769-dc22
A full catalogue record for this book is available from
the British Library.

Acknowledgements
We would like to thank the following for permission to
reproduce photographs: Belfast Print Works p. 13; © Capstone
Global Library Ltd p. 10 (Tudor Photography); © Capstone
Publishers pp. 8, 20, 21, 22 left, 22 right, 23 – transfer
(Karon Dubke); © Corbis p. 16 (Michael S. Wertz); Corbis
p. 9 (© Penny Tweedie), 11 (© Philadelphia Museum of Art);
M.C. Escher's "Development II" © 2010 The M.C. Escher
Company- Holland. All rights reserved www.mcescher.com
p. 19; Photolibrary p. 7 (John Warburton-Lee Photography/
John Warburton-Lee); Scala p. 17 (Museum of Modern Art,
New York); Shutterstock pp. 4 (© Katrina Brown), 15, 23 –
abstract (© Elena Ray), 23 – texture (© Konstantin Sutyagin),
23 – textile (© afaizal), 23 – surface (© Evgenia Sh.), 23 –
subject (© Nastenok), 23– gallery (© Shamleen); The Bridge-
man Art Library pp. 5 (Haags Gemeentemuseum, The Hague,
Netherlands), 6 (© Fry Art Gallery, Saffron Walden, Essex,
UK), 12 (© The British Sporting Art Trust/Private Collection),
14 (© Christie's Images), 18 (Private Collection).

Front cover photograph of 18th-century head of a woman by
Kitagawa Utamaro reproduced with permission of Corbis (©
The Gallery Collection). Back cover photograph of children's
hand prints reproduced with permission of Shutterstock (©
Katrina Brown). Back cover photograph of rolling paint over
a leaf reproduced with permission of © Capstone Publishers
(Karon Dubke).

Every effort has been made to contact copyright holders
of material reproduced in this book. Any omissions will
be rectified in subsequent printings if notice is given to
the publisher.

All the Internet addresses (URLs) given in this book were valid
at the time of going to press. However, due to the dynamic
nature of the Internet, some addresses may have changed, or
sites may have changed or ceased to exist since publication.
While the author and publisher regret any inconvenience this
may cause readers, no responsibility for any such changes can
be accepted by either the author or the publisher.

Contents

Some words are shown in bold, **like this**. You can find out what they mean by looking in the glossary.

What is a print?

A print is the mark you make when you cover something in paint and press it on to paper.

You can use printing to make the same mark again and again.

Some artists use printing to make pictures.

They can print many copies of the same picture.

Where can I see prints?

Museums collect prints from different times and places.

Some prints made by artists are displayed in **galleries**.

textile prints

You can see prints all around
you, too.

People use printing to decorate
textiles and many other things.

What do people use to make prints?

You can dip an object in paint and press it on to a flat **surface**.

You can print shapes on a soft surface such as clay.

Artists scratch, carve, or draw a picture on to a special surface.

They use printing to **transfer** the picture on to a new surface, such as paper.

How do people make block prints?

Have you ever made potato prints?
This is a kind of block printing.

Artists carve a design into a block
made from wood or another material.

They cover the block in ink and press it on to paper or fabric.

This print of a Japanese lady was made over 200 years ago.

How do people use texture in prints?

Prints can look very different from drawings and paintings.

This print uses **texture** to show shiny horses, rough ground, and stormy weather.

This picture was printed from
a collage.

The artist used different textures to
show the cockerel's feathers.

What do prints show?

Some artists make prints of real things, such as animals.

This print shows the **texture** of wrinkly rhino skin.

Some artists make **abstract** prints to show ideas and feelings.

What do the shapes in this picture make you think and feel?

How can prints show ideas and feelings?

Artists use colours, shapes, and **textures** to tell us about their **subject**.

Flat shapes and bright colours make these people look happy and lively.

This print has jagged lines and
no colours.

Do you think the person feels happy,
angry, sad, or scared?

How do people use pattern in prints?

The same marks can be printed many times to make a pattern.

Printing is used to decorate pottery, wallpaper, and **textiles**.

Artists use patterns in their
pictures, too.

Shapes turn into lizards in this print.

Start to print!

The print on page 13 is made from a collage. You can make one, too!

1. Collect materials with interesting **textures**. Use things that you might throw away, such as sponge, **textile** scraps, corrugated card, and leaves.

2. Arrange the materials to make a collage picture of an animal.

3. When you are happy with your design, glue the materials on to a piece of thick card. Make sure that they are all about the same height.

4. Use a roller to cover your collage in ink.

5. Put a sheet of paper over the inked collage. Roll a clean roller over the paper to make a print.

6. You can make more copies of your picture by doing steps 4 and 5 again.

Glossary

abstract type of art where the shapes and colours show ideas and feelings instead of real things

gallery place where art is displayed for people to look at

subject person, place, or object shown in a piece of art

surface something that an artist prints on, such as paper, card, clay, fabric, or wood

textile material or fabric, used to make clothes and other things

texture how a surface looks and feels

transfer move something from one place to another. Printing moves a picture from one surface to another.

Find out more

Websites

See all the different ways to make prints on this website:
www.moma.org/interactives/projects/2001/whatisaprint/print.html

Print your own wallpaper design on this website:
www.vam.ac.uk/vastatic/microsites/1185_families/flash/

Index